No Sand in the House!

Written by Jennifer L. Crawford   Illustrated by Hannah Tuohy

For Mom & Dad With Love-J.C.   For G&G Love -H

Library of Congress Control Number: 2013908493
ISBN 978-0-615-81199-4
Printed in the United States of America.
10 9 8 7 6 5 4 3 2 1

For Abby, summer was the best season of all.

The rest of her family had their favorite seasons. In the spring, her Mom shed her wool sweaters and heavy boots to garden and smell flowers in the air.

Her Dad preferred snowboarding and sledding in the snowy winter months.

Abby's little brother, Charlie, could sit in fall leaves for hours with just his imagination and without a care in the world.

But Abby loved summer. School was out, for one thing, but the best thing about summer for Abby was spending weeks at a time with her grandparents at the Shore.

In fact, Abby loved everything about the Shore. She loved building sand castles and looking for shells.

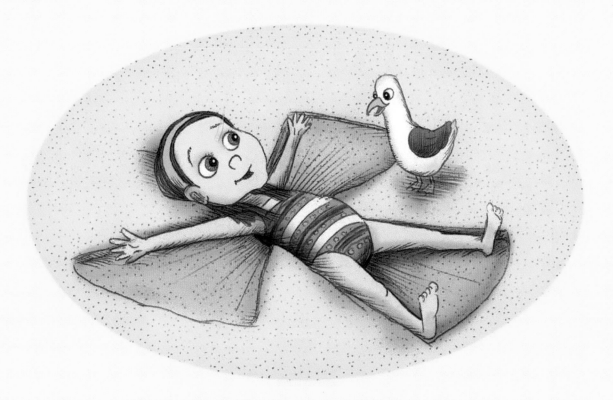

She loved digging for sand crabs and dredging up seaweed.

She loved playing bakery and making sand pastries for her family.

Mostly, she loved spending time with her Pop-Pop, who adored spending time with her —except for one small thing, actually lots of very small things.

Every summer, without fail, before Abby even took
one step inside the Shore house, Pop-Pop asked,
"What's Rule #1?"
"Don't panic?" guessed Abby.

"No," Pop-Pop said with a disappointed frown.
"Rule #1 is: No sand in the house."
Offering a second chance, Pop-Pop hopefully
quizzed, "What's Rule #2?"
Abby shrugged.

"Rule #2 is: No sand in the house."
"But, Pop-Pop, that's the same as Rule #1,"
cried Abby indignantly.

During morning strolls on the beach, Pop-Pop always carried the bucket while Abby filled it to the rim with beach glass and shells. He never once complained, even if she already had several full buckets back at the house. But as soon as they returned home to the creaky screen door, Pop-Pop reminded Abby, "No sand in the house."

During afternoon walks to the ice cream shop, where Abby always ordered more than her parents would have allowed, Pop-Pop swung Abby in his arms and laughed at her stories.

But, sure enough, when they reached that creaky screen door, Pop-Pop muttered, "No sand in the house."

Every summer Abby walked the 217 steps to the top of the lighthouse. Pop-Pop shared in her delight and pride, but only after making sure there would be, "No sand in the house."

Even when they visited the amusement park or Abby's favorite restaurant for a grilled pizza sandwich—places that weren't even near the beach—upon their return, Pop-Pop would inevitably grumble, "No sand in the house."

When Abby was old enough, it became her job to teach Charlie Rule #1 and Rule #2. In this one thing, above all others, they put their bickering aside and worked as a team.

They scrubbed. They hosed. They tried everything!

They even thought about wearing socks and shoes,
but decided that wasn't a very "beachy" thing to do.

Abby and Charlie struggled to keep every grain of sand
outside. It was impossible. Sand hid everywhere.

What were the consequences of bringing sand into the house? They did not want to be the ones to find out. Until one day, they did.

Seasons changed. Months passed. Halloween approached. And so did a hurricane.

Abby lay in bed at night listening to her parents whisper. She didn't know exactly what a hurricane could do, but it must be serious if her parents whispered about it.

Day after day, school was canceled. Abby felt the rain and the wind at her house. Was this same rain and wind affecting Pop-Pop?

Night after night, Abby heard the
hushed whispers and stifled tears from
her parents. In the morning her
Mom's eyes were red and puffy.

Then without warning, the rains stopped. Even
though it wasn't summer, Abby knew from
listening to the whispers and the late-night phone
calls that it was time to head to the Shore.

The family drove straight to Pop-Pop's house, but along the way, nothing looked the same. Patio furniture and plastic trash bins littered the pebble-covered lawns. Fences lay knocked down; muck covered everything. Disorder reigned.

It didn't look like the Shore Abby
knew from memory.

Abby could barely see Pop-Pop through the
old creaky screen door.

Abby entered first. Her mouth dropped
open, but before she could speak . . .

"Pop-Pop," blurted Charlie.
"There's sand in the house!"

Pop-Pop took a deep breath. He closed his eyes. His face glowed sun-burned red while his cheeks filled like balloons. And then, without warning—

—he made a sound. Was it a cry? A gasp? A snort?
Could it be—a laugh? Yes!

And once it started, it didn't stop. Within seconds, all three
of them laughed harder than they had in a long time.

As Pop-Pop hugged them tight, Abby knew that it wasn't
just love in his arms but the promise of lazy beach days and
cool ice cream nights for many summers to come
. . . even with quite a bit of sand in the house.

Author Jennifer Crawford grew up in New Jersey and attended Boston College, while managing to spend her summers at Long Beach Island, NJ. Though she loves to travel, she is just as happy at home in Virginia with her family and their pet hermit crabs. She returns to the Jersey Shore each summer and finds it impossibly difficult to follow Rule #1.

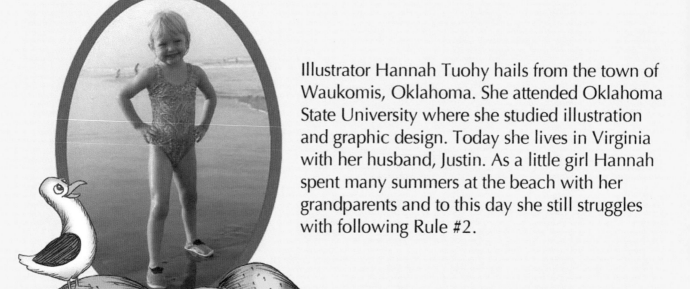

Illustrator Hannah Tuohy hails from the town of Waukomis, Oklahoma. She attended Oklahoma State University where she studied illustration and graphic design. Today she lives in Virginia with her husband, Justin. As a little girl Hannah spent many summers at the beach with her grandparents and to this day she still struggles with following Rule #2.

A portion of the proceeds from the sale of this book will be donated to organizations that are helping to rebuild the Jersey Shore after the destruction caused by Hurricane Sandy in 2012.
Please visit www.nosandinthehouse.com for more information about these charitable organizations.